Gypsy Rose

a historical fiction

a novel

by

Maric Garcia

April Camp NaNoWriMo Winner 2019

I went through four different goals: 1). 15,000 (didn't feel right); 2) 10,000 (still didn't feel right); 3) 5,000 (felt right and I hit that goal quickly); 4 & final) 7,500 (reached rather quickly). All in all, very proud of this novel.

Specialty Novels

2030

Writing Death

Black Widow

Marvelous

Sai

Statement from the Author

I got the idea for this novel after I learned of Gypsy Rose from Hulu's The Act. I felt sorry for this girl—young woman—who had been abused by her mother. I think that her sentence should be reduced.

This poor girl has suffered enough. Yes, I understand that she planned the death of her mother, but her mother was cruel. Sick. They both needed help. Her mother was too sick to ask for it and Gypsy was too scared to.

Disclaimer

While the events that inspired this novel are
true, the events in this novel are fiction.

Dedication

To those who are abused and battered.

Introduction:

I am Gypsy Rose

My name is Gypsy Rose Blanchard and I'm twenty years old. I have been confined to a wheelchair and told that I had leukemia by my mother. DeeDee Blanchard. My father wasn't in my life. I only saw him a handful of times. Him and my stepmother.

I was born in July of 1991 and very healthy. According to my mother; however, that changed when I was seven years old. I had been in a car accident and scraped my knee. From then on, I was confined to the wheelchair. I didn't need it.

This is my story. I will expose my mother's lies. Finally.

I will get the happy ending that I crave.

That I deserve.

Please listen and tell me what you think.

Chapter One:

The First Lie

My mother told me that my father wanted nothing to do with me and never sent her any money to help. That was a lie. Now that I'm free, I found out the truth. He called her often to speak with me and she always told him that I was sick or not available.

In fact, I was. All the time. She never let me out of her sight unless she was napping. She wouldn't even let me hang out with the neighbor, Laci on our own front porch.

My mother was extremely jealous and possessive of me. I wasn't allowed to have friends or a phone, laptop, or Facebook page of my own. I had to hide these and many other things from her.

It was like I was several different people. I was the loving, devoted daughter to the mother that always cared for me; I was the girl that guys wanted. The friend that was always there to listen. Deep down all I wanted to do was break free from my mother and be my own person. Instead, I was forced to lie to celebrities and charities and neighbors about my illnesses.

Now, don't get me wrong, I knew that I could walk and that I could eat without a feeding tube, but I was extremely scared of my mother. If I disobeyed her, and she caught me, there were consequences. There were times, especially after the age of eleven, that I was bound to my bed. Sometimes for days. She would also deprive me of food and water. Just because I done something that I didn't want to do.

I hated lying to everyone. She would beat me as well. One time, when she found my laptop, she threw me on my bed. She choked me and tried to tie me up. I kneed her and she let me go.

I tried to leave then, but she was crying for me and stayed. I should have left then.

I wanted to run away so badly. Maybe I suffered from Stockholm Syndrome. I mean, she was my mother. Why was she like that?

The second lie was that I had leukemia and muscular dystrophy; among other diseases. She would bathe me and shave my head constantly, to keep up the appearance that I was going through chemo treatments.

Third lie? That the medication that I was taking was needed. It caused all of my teeth to become like Swiss cheese! I thought that it had been the sweets that I was sneaking at night. My mother had told me that I had an allergy to sugar and I wanted to put it to the test. When I found out that I didn't have that allergy, I went a bit overboard. I had found out that I was the medications. I had to have all of my teeth pulled at nearly eighteen years old!

The fourth lie? Well, that was that bad. My mother told me that she loved me. Why was that a lie? Simply because if she had loved me, then she never would have lied to me in the first place.

If my mother loved me, as she had claimed, why would she tell me that I was dying? Why would she lie about my age and how smart I was?

My mother told me that I was born in 1993 and then changed it to 1995. She also told me and others, that I had the mental compacity of a seven-year-old.

What seven-year-old as sexual urges in the way that I did? Can someone, anyone, please tell me that?

I know that I loved my mother, even though I was scared of her. I know that when I found out that she had to take insulin, that I was worried she was going to die.

I think she used that to keep me with her.

Chapter Two:

My Secrets

When I was "seventeen" I stole money that my mother had hidden. It was money that I had "earned" by playing my part as the infantile, paraplegic little girl. I had stolen our neighbors and others' hearts.

My mother had me do some shopping one day, when she wasn't feeling well. I bought myself a laptop with the money that I had stolen. I'd also purchased a cellphone that I was able to hide.

The only reason that she had found the laptop was that I had fallen asleep on the floor next to it. She was livid when she discovered it.

I had been talking to a boy named Nick that I had met on a Christian dating site. My neighbor had told me about it. She had met her boyfriend on there as well. Nick seemed wonderful.

He liked me even after he discovered that I was confined to a wheelchair and had no hair. He told me that he would love me no matter what.

Nick wasn't my first boyfriend; I had met someone and ran away to be with him. I don't like to talk about him. It hurts. My mother lied to him and told him that I was fifteen years old and that if he told me that he didn't want me, that she wouldn't go to the police.

Nothing had happened with him. Nothing except a very sweet kiss. He had sent me a wig. A red one. I loved it.

So, my secrets were plenty. I knew that I could walk, like I said. I knew that. I also knew that I could eat, like I said. She would pretend that I couldn't eat and blend my food and give it to me through a feeding tube that was unnecessary.

I had had so many unnecessary surgeries. I did have some hate in my heart for my mother. Why would any mother do that? I guess; however, that it could have been worse. She could have killed me outright.

Like Susan Smith had done to her boys or Andrea Yates.

Though I think that would have been better than living the way that I did. My mother taught me to steal and lie. I hated that. I hated lying.

Chapter Three:

The Big Reveal

There are more things to come, but I had to speak of this before the end of my narrative. This was the most important thing that I had ever done.

I think that if I hadn't freed myself this way, that I would have either killed my mother or had someone else do it for me. Like Nick. He would have killed for me. I know he would have. He had already offered to do so.

We even had a plan. Nick would come over after my mother had gone to bed and then stabbed her. I had hidden a knife and some duct tape near her room so that we could do it.

I don't think, that as much as I hated my situation and my mother, that I would have been able to actually carry out the murder. I also don't think that Nick would have let me.

Though I think in the end he would have thrown me under the bus. Saying that I planned the whole thing.

I'm glad that we aren't together anymore. Our relationship didn't last long once I was away from my mother. I think, in some ways, he was like her. Manipulative. Needy.

He was my first true, sexual experience. I thought I was in love with him. Totally and completely. I would have done anything for him. Even spend time in prison, if that situation every occurred. Thankfully, it didn't.

* * *

"Mama," I said. "I can't take this anymore."

"What are you going on about Gypsy Rose?" my mother asked, whispering. "You know what will happen."

17

"I don't care. I want to be with Nick. I am an adult and I can make my own choices. You can't control me forever."

"Oh, yes, sweetheart, I can."

I looked over my shoulder at her. "No, you can't. I can end this right now. I can expose all of your lies. I *will* expose all of your lies. I have been keeping proof of your atrocities to those charities and to me. Proof that I was going along with it."

"Gyspy Rose..."

"Then say its okay to be with him."

"No. *I* need you more than he does. I am sick."

"I know that, but you are an adult and as your child, I should not have to take care of you. You preached to me about the allergies to sweets, but maybe your diabetes is God's way of saying that *you're* allergic to sweets."

"What brought all of this on?"

"Its been coming for a long time. First with Scott, you EMBARASSED ME by lying to him. Then you beat me when we got home. You've forced me to live my life in an un-needed wheelchair and feeding tube!"

We were outside on our front porch.

"Stop this! I forbid it!"

My mother's voice was getting louder and louder. More hysterical with each octave it went up and our neighbors were starting to come out of their homes to see what was going on.

I looked her dead in the eyes and said, "You can't stop me anymore."

I wheeled myself down the ramp that Habitat Humanity had built for just for me in the house that was built just for us and into the middle of the street.

"Everyone, can I have your attention please?" I called out.

"Gyspy, no!" my mother hollered.

"No, Mama. It's time for the lies to stop."

"What lies?" Laci, my neighbor and friend, asked. She was coming towards me, face full of concern. "Is everything okay?"

"No, Laci, its not."

"What's going on?"

"My mother is a liar."

19

"Gypsy, that's not a nice thing to say."

"Its true. I'll show you."

"GYPSY!!!!" I could hear my mother running towards me.

I stood up and walked the rest of the way to Laci. I saw the surprise on her face. "W-what? You can walk?"

"Yes. My mother forced me to stay in that chair for my whole life. I also found out that I am not eighteen; I'm nineteen, almost twenty. She lied to me about everything. I am not sick and I never was."

"If you knew, why did you go along with it?" another neighbor asked. I think it was Laci's mother, M.J.

"When I was younger, I did believe it. Why would my mother lie to me about something like that? Why would any mother force her healthy, vibrant daughter to live her life confined to a wheelchair with an expiration date looming? Why would a mother do that?"

"You didn't answer the question, Gypsy Rose," a third neighbor asked

Gypsy Rose   Marie Garcia

"Once I was older, I kept going along with it because I was scared."

"Why?"

"She beats me. Sometimes, if I try to leave, she will chain me to my bed or tie me up. Sometimes, she will not give me any food. For days."

"What?"

"I am sorry that I lied to all of you, you have all been so wonderful to me. Accepting of my conditions."

"She has to pay for what she's done."

I looked at my mother as she stopped at the edge of the driveway. "She will."

21

Chapter Four:

Meeting Nick in Person

That was so awesome, right?! There's more to that later. Right now, I want to speak about meting Nick in person and online for the first time.

The first time we met online, was when I bought my laptop. I had a brown wig and wore it in a loose, side-ponytail with a ribbon wrapped around it.

I used that as my profile picture for that Christian dating site. I received, like, ten responses! I clicked on Nick's message and we started chatting. He told me that I was beautiful and reminded him of a Princess. I told him that Rapunzel was my favorite Disney Princess after he had told me that his cousin liked *Tangled*. He said I was prettier than Rapunzel.

I liked that. It made me feel special. Special in a good way and not the way my mother was intending.

We spoke nearly every night for a week before we did a video chat for the first time. That's when I told him that I had to use a wheelchair and that I was bald.

Nick told me that he would love me no matter what and that my illnesses and circumstances wouldn't change the way he felt about me.

We had a plan to meet in person.

* * *

"Mama?" I asked.

"Yes, sweet-pea?" my mother replied.

"Do you think we could go to see *Cinderella*?"

"Of course, Gypsy Rose. When?"

"I think it's tomorrow."

"Sure. You know how I love Cinderella."

"Yes, Mama."

"Look at the time. We should get to bed."

"Yes, Mama."

I rolled myself to my room and she helped me into the bed and helped me put my CPAP mask on. Again, it wasn't necessary. None of it.

Nick was going to meet us at the movies. My mother didn't know that. The plan was to accidentally run into him and then have him sit with us during the movie.

We had been talking for a few months. I just hoped that it went well.

The next afternoon, we arrived at the movie theater and I couldn't see inside the building. I was hoping that Nick was already there, waiting at the concession stand. Better yet, outside.

Mother bought our tickets, telling the clerk that I was twelve to get the children's discount. He wasn't there.

I was suddenly nervous. My mother had dressed me up as Cinderella. Complete with blond wig and the slippers.

We entered the building and I still couldn't see him. I bet he looked so cute in the sapphire blue button down shirt that I had sent him.

Brown hair and tall. Of course, anyone was tall next to me at the moment.

"Can I have some popcorn, Mama?" I asked. "Some water?"

"Sure," she said. "A small one."

"Great."

She wheeled me over and Nick wasn't there. Mama had walked up to the counter and ordered some water and popcorn.

I twirled and he still wasn't there.

"Gypsy?" he asked. He was here. I was so close to crying.

"Yes?" My stomach was full of butterflies. "Do I know you?"

"I've seen you on TV and you look so pretty."

"Thank you."

"What movie are you going to see?"

"*Cinderella*."

"Me, too. I'm Nick."

"Nice to meet you. This is my mother, DeeDee."

"Charmed," my mother said. She didn't sound happy. "What do you want?"

"Can you sit with us?"

"Sure."

"Oh, sweetheart, I don't know if that's a good idea."

"How come?"

"Well, we don't know this young man."

"I know, but we could get to know him. He's a fan." I knew how to drive this home by beckoning her close, whispering, "He may have money on him."

"Please, do sit with us."

"Thank you, ma'am."

"Mama, can you take our picture?"

"Sure."

We smiled big. It would be the only picture of us.

We got settled and then I started chatting with Nick, "learning" about him for the "first time" as far as my mother was concerned. I could tell that she wasn't happy that he was with us.

Suddenly, my mother moved us away and every time that Nick would move with us, she moved us again.

Finally, I asked to go to the restroom after noticing that Nick had left.

"Oh…" my mother said.

"I can go by myself. I could get you some more popcorn," I said.

"Sure. Sure. Be quick."

"Okay."

I had looked for Nick in the hallway and he wasn't there. Finally, he was coming out of the restroom and I motioned for him to go to the family restroom further down the hall.

I wheeled myself there and entered, he soon followed.

We had sex on the floor of the family restroom. It was my first time and it was nice.

Chapter Five:

Arriving Home

When we got home that night, there was huge fight.

"You're a whore!" my mother bellowed. "I need you! You'd rather be with some boy!"

"I'm not a whore, mother! I just met him!" I yelled back.

This was well before my big reveal. Maybe a month or so before.

"I don't think so. I know you've been sneaking out of bed to use a laptop. Where did you get that?"

"None of your business."

"Oh, what you do, whore, is my business."

"I am not a child and you need to stop treating me like one."

"In the eyes of the law, you *are* a child!"

"I don't care. I will run away if I have to."

"OH? Where would you go? How would you get there?"

"I would find my father. Tell him what's really been going on here. Tell him how you treat me."

"Does he ever call you? Do we ever see one cent from that man?"

"He's my father!"

"He's a louse. A cad! Stay away from him!!"

"I will not! Not any longer!'

She rushed me before I could react and wheel or jump out of her way. My mother pulled me out of my chair and she ran down the hallway with me. Dragging me by the scruff of my neck.

"Stop! Help! Someone please help me!"

"No one will come to help you. No one cares!"

"Someone will come."

"No, they won't."

She threw me onto the bed and tied me up. There were handcuffs that she had fixed to the headboard. I hated this bed.

"You can stay here and think about what you did."

Then she walked out and left me there for nearly a week.

* * *

The following Monday, my mother had finally returned to my room. She helped me out of the bed and let me walk to the bathroom. She stripped me and then helped me into the tub.

"Stay here," she said. "I need to go remove your bedding and throw it all into the laundry machine."

"Yes, Mama," I said, sullenly. My legs hurt from not being able to move. My arms hurt from not being able to move.

"We have to go to the doctor today and get that feeding tube taken care of."

"Yes, Mama."

"So filthy."

I will admit that I wanted her dead after this past week. It was awful. She didn't feed me, actual food or through the feeding tube; she left me to sit in my own feces and urine for seven days.

I couldn't believe that it happened. She usually at least lets me go to the restroom. Even if she has a potty chair.

She had returned from the bedroom and tossing the laundry in. Then she cleaned me up.

"Good, no bed sores, "she said, inspecting my body. "Don't need those pesky doctors asking unnecessary questions."

"Like I my age?"

"Watch your mouth."

I glared at her and flinched when she raised her hand to me.

"You can't hit me or you'll have to explain it to the doctors."

"Bitch."

"Maybe, but so are you."

She finished washing me and then helped me out. She dressed me up and put me back into the chair.

We left and I so wanted to tell the doctor to go ahead and remove the tube, but she rarely leaves me alone with the doctor or the nurse. She does all of the talking. Even now.

More especially now. Since I could talk and left my thoughts and feelings be better known now.

Man, I hated her a lot.

Chapter Six:

Speaking to Nick

When I was finally able to be alone. It was at night and I made sure that she was asleep before I left my bed and checked anything on my phone.

I still hadn't been able to replace my laptop.

I checked my phone and there were about thirty messages from Nick.

Are you okay?

What did she say?

Are you okay?

I'm still in town, can we meet up without your mother?

ARE YOU OKAY?????

Gypsy?!?

I'm calling the police.

Many more messages before and after those.

I called him. "I'm sorry!" I said. "Don't call the police, I'm okay."

"Gypsy? What the fuck happened?" he demanded.

"She chained me to the bed."

He gasped. "Are you sure you're okay? You don't need me to call the police?"

"No. I'm reaching the end of my rope though. I am ready to reveal the truth about my mother."

"Where will you go?"

"I went through her phone. I found my father's number. I'm going to call him. Tell him what's going on."

"Will he tell your mother?"

"I'm going to ask him not to and to see if he can meet me one night while she's out of the house."

"She leaves you alone?"

"Sometimes. Never for very long though."

34

"Okay. Can you sneak out?"

"Come by the house and I can meet you outback."

"Okay. I will be there soon."

"Be quiet and I'll watch for you by the back door."

"Great. See you soon, love you."

"Love you."

While I waited for Nick, I called my father.

"Hello?" he asked, picking up on the second ring. "Who is this?"

"Daddy?" I said, quietly. "It's Gypsy Rose."

"Gypsy?!"

"Yes."

"Are you okay? Is DeeDee? Why are you whispering?"

"Mama doesn't know I'm calling you. I'm calling from a phone that I bought secretly. She's been lying to you Daddy. I can walk and I'm not sick. Come by the house next week, don't tell Mama. I'll show you that she's lying."

"Okay. I don't like not telling your mother."

"Does she tell you everything?"

"No."

"See you next week, Daddy. I love you. Please don't tell her about this phone or our conversation."

"Okay. I will see you soon. I love you."

"I know. I'm sorry that it's taken until now for us to be able to speak."

"She told me you were busy."

"I know. Bye."

I hung up and watched for Nick.

Chapter Seven:

Meeting My Father

I found away to be away from my mother long enough to meet up with my father before revealing the truth.

"Daddy?" I asked. There was a man standing around the corner from the house and he nodded.

"Gypsy?" he asked, unsure.

Surely my mother had sent pictures of me to him, at least.

"Yes. We have some time to talk before I reveal everything to everyone."

"What's going on?" I stood up and walked towards my father. He rushed to me. "Should you be doing that?"

"I can walk, Daddy. Nothing Mama said is true. I'm not sick. I can walk."

"Truly?"

"Yes. Before I reveal everything, I want to know if I can come live with you. I don't want to reveal the truth and then end up back with her and being beaten."

"Of course, you can. I never would have left you with her. I didn't know."

"She told me that you never sent any money."

"I did. Every month. $1,200 every month."

I believed him. "I believe you, Daddy. I am doing this because I'm scared that I will do something to her."

"You can come home with me. I'm going to call your stepmother. Explain to her what's going on. When are you revealing this?"

"Soon. Next hour or so."

"Okay. Give me an hour. I want her get a room ready for you and explain that you aren't sick."

"Thank you."

"You're my daughter. I would do anything for you."

"I love you, Daddy."

"I love you, too, Gypsy Rose. My beautiful daughter."

I smiled and got back into my chair and wheeled myself back to the house.

When I got home, I started the fight that led us to our confrontation outside and revealing the truth to our neighbors.

* * *

"Hello?" my father said, walking towards. "Gypsy Rose?"

"Daddy?" I asked. I had asked him prior to meeting him to pretend that he was learning things for the first time. "I want to live with you."

"No!" my mother bellowed.

"Who are you?" Laci asked.

"I'm her father."

"You're the deadbeat?"

"I paid DeeDee $1,200 a month in child support. I can show anyone the checks in my book. Or the statement from my bank. I am taking Gypsy home with me."

"No!"

My father glared at my mother. "We will be back tomorrow to get her things. Pack up what she doesn't need right away and have it shipped to my home. Pack what she needs immediately."

I took my father's hand and we headed down the street to his car.

Once I was in his car, I turned back. My neighbors were staring at my mother's back as she headed back into the house.

Chapter Eight:

Finding My Mother

That night, I talked to my stepmother.

"Hello?" I asked, timidly.

"Hello, darlin," my stepmother, Kristy, said. "I'm your stepmom. I don't know if you remember me or not."

"Kind of. I'm sorry!'

"It's okay. Don't worry about it. We only met a few times and they weren't long visits. I can't wait for you to come home with your Daddy. Your brother and sister can't wait to meet you either."

"I have a brother and sister?"

Kristy chuckled. "Dylan and Mia. We can't wait for you to be a real part of our family."

"I can't wait either. I have a question."

"Sure, sweetie."

"Do I call you Kristy or Mom?"

"Whatever you want. Whatever you're comfortable with. Let me talk to your Daddy and we'll see you soon."

"Okay. Bye!"

"Bye."

I handed the phone to my father and crawled into bed. I fell asleep, exhausted.

* * *

The next day, we had the back of his rented truck filled with boxed. I didn't think we would need that many.

I just wanted to get some stuffed animals that I had and some clothes.

I didn't want anything else from the house. I wanted a fresh start.

I walked up to the front door and knocked.

"Gypsy?" Laci called.

"Hi, Laci," I called back. "Have you seen my mother?"

"Not since you left yesterday. I don't think she locked the door."

"Okay."

I opened the door and walked in. I liked that. Walking and not wheeling in.

"Mama?" I called.

"DeeDee?" my father called out.

No answer.

"I'll look for her. Go ahead and get your things."

"I don't need a lot, Daddy. I just want to get some clothes and some personal items. Mama's room is across from mine. Just down the hall."

He followed me down the hallway and my mother's door was closed. "She maybe sleeping. Let me go get her."

I opened her door without knocking and she was lying on the bed. "Mama?" I said. "I'm here to get my things. Mama?"

"DeeDee?" my father said, standing behind me.

I walked towards the bed and shook her. "Mama? Mama? Daddy??"

He came into the room and pushed me aside. "DeeDee? God, she's freezing. Call 911!"

I grabbed my mother's phone off the table next to her bed and quickly called 911. I gave them my address and told them to just come on in.

"Is she breathing?" the operator asked.

"No. I don't think so. My father said she's cold."

"We've got help on the way. Stay on the line please."

"Okay."

"Can you tell me what happened?"

"I walked away from her last night."

"Are there medicines in the house?"

"Yes. A bunch."

"Do you see any pill bottles or things like that near her?"

"No. I just came in, shook her, and then had my Daddy take a look at her. He said she was cold and told me to call you."

I started to cry. "Do you think she's okay?"

"Sweetie…"

"Oh, no."

I dropped the phone and leaned against the wall.

Chapter Nine:

Apologizing to Laci

Laci was sitting beside me on the lawn of her house. "Are you okay?" she asked.

"I never should have left her," I said, guiltily. "This is all my fault."

"No, sweetie. It's your mother's fault. She never should have done those things to you. Ultimately, it was your mother's guilt that lead her to do this. That's what the note said."

"I know."

My mother had left a suicide note in the kitchen next to the bottles of oxytocin that she had taken.

In it she had said that she didn't blame me and that she was surprised that she hadn't driven me away a long time ago. She had been waiting for me to leave her.

She apologized for her treatment of me and told the police that would no doubt be investing her lies that she had money to pay back everyone that she had lied to.

My mother had taken full responsibility for what she had done. Told them that I had no knowledge of anything, no matter what I had said.

The coroner said that he would be removing her body soon and thought that I shouldn't be there when he did it.

Laci took me to her place and we sat on the lawn.

"I'm so sorry, Laci," I said, looking at her. "I know I should have said something sooner. I was just so scared."]

"I understand, Gypsy," she said, hugging me slightly. "None of us blame you."

"I wanted to tell you; I have a boyfriend. I know this isn't the best time to mention it. I've been wanting to tell you since I met him. He's really nice. I met him on that dating site you told me about."

"That's great. Have you met in person yet?"

"Yeah. We met at the new *Cinderella* movie. We've been talking for a very long time and thought it was time to meet in person. We just had to convince my mother that he was a good man."

"Did you?"

"No. She didn't like him at all."

"Well, mother's want to protect us."

"I know. He did come off a little creepy. I don't think I'm going to see him again though."

"How come?"

"We hooked up in the restroom and I wasn't as attracted to him as I thought I would be. We've done video chats."

"But meeting in person is very different than video chat."

"Yes."

"I can understand that."

"Once I finally get to my Dad's, I'm going to tell him."

"Good. Don't wait too long."

"I won't. I'm going to miss you, Laci. You've been a true friend and like a big sister to me."

"I'm going to miss you, too. I'm glad to have known you, Ms. Gypsy Rose Blanchard. Good luck in life."

"Thank you. You, too. I'll try to write once I get settled and then give you my new number."

"Of course." Laci looked over to my house. "Don't look, Gypsy. They're removing your mother."

I did look and I felt shame and guilt.

I shouldn't have. I was old enough to make my own decisions and she'd left me no choice.

Chapter Ten:

Candlelight Vigil?

Before I left town with my father, I asked if it would be okay to hold a candlelight vigil for my mother.

"If you think people will attend," he said. "I don't want you to be disappointed if no one shows up."

"Do you think they won't?" I asked. I hadn't even considered that.

"Probably not. Your neighbors are really upset that she lied."

"Oh. Good point. Okay, we can go then. I don't think it would be right to have one if no one will show up. Its really just for me anyway."

"Are you feeling guilty?"

"A little bit."

"Sweetie, she did this to herself. She was sick."

"I know. I feel like if I hadn't told the truth, she'd still be alive."

"Maybe, but you did what you did to save yourself. That's a good thing. Admirable, if you ask me. Brave, too."

"You think so?"

"Yes, I do."

After my mother had been removed and they had completed their investigation of the house and property, I was able to get back into the house and gather some things up.

Tomorrow we'd be at his home.

* * *

After my father had gone to bed, we'd stayed in a motel that first night, in case the police needed something; my phone buzzed.

It was Nick.

I had been dreading this.

"Hi," he texted. *"R u ok?"*

We hadn't had a chance to speak, really, since the day we met at the movie theater and had, had sex.

"Not really," I replied. *"My mom killed herself last night."*

"Did she hurt u?"

"No. I told everyone the truth and when I returned home this morning she was dead. Pills."

"OMG. Now we can be together!"

I sighed quietly. I didn't want to wake my father up. *"No, we can't."*

"Y not?"

"I am moving away with my father. I don't like you like that anymore."

"What?! R u serious?"

"Yes."

"We fucked and now u don't "like me like that anymore?" What the fuck?"

"Just leave me alone."

"No. U r mine."

"No, I'm not. This phone is going to be destroyed. I'm closing my email and Facebook accounts."

"Gypsy…"

"No."

I shut my phone off and then took it outside and threw it into the pool. I was done with Nick and he needed to realize that.

Chapter Eleven:

Stalker

I had been with my dad for about a month when I started getting strange letters in the mail. I also started getting strange calls on my new cellphone and emails through my new email and Facebook accounts.

No one had these things except for Laci, my dad, stepmom, and brother and sister. I hadn't even really made any friends yet.

I went to my Dad.

"Dad, those letters I've been getting, I haven't given out the address to anyone," I said. "I'm very concerned."

"What do the letters say?" he asked.

I had kept them and handed them all to hm. "I'm also getting phone calls and emails. Messages on Facebook. No one has that but you, Kristy, Mia, and Dylan. Laci. That's it. You can go on there and look."

"No friend from school or anything?"

"I get a few requests from people, but I don't know them. I don't accept them."

"Good for you. Well, I'll look into those things. Let me know if you get anymore."

"Okay. I keep all of the messages I'm sent. I printed them off and also saved each one with a timestamp and the user."

"Okay. Make me copies and I'll take it to the police."

I nodded and went to get them out of my room. "Here you go."

"I'll go right now. Maybe they can find out where they're coming from."

"Thank you."

I had a job interview tomorrow and one the next day. I couldn't do much and I knew that, but I didn't think it would hurt to try. All they could tell me what no.

"Are you looking forward to your interviews?" Kristy asked, coming into the room.

"Yeah, I am," I said, smiling at her. She was everything that I had wished my mother had been. Kind, caring, loving. "Are you still going to take me?"

"Yes, ma'am."

"Great. Do you think that some time this week that one of you could teach me to drive? I signed up for the classes."

"Sure. As a matter of fact, we'll leave a little early tomorrow and go practice in a nearby parking lot."

"Really?"

"Yes."

"Yay!" I jumped up and down, clapping my hands and gave her a hug. "Thank you!"

She laughed and wrapped her arms around my waist. "Anytime, sweetie."

"Gypsy?" my brother asked.

"Yeah, Mason?"

"I'm glad you're here."

I smiled. "Me, too."

"You'll make some friends soon, Gypsy," Mia, my sister, said. "I know it."

"Thank you. I hope so."

She smiled at me and we headed out back to play on the trampoline.

* * *

Just before bed, my phone rang. "Hello?" I asked.

I didn't look at the caller ID, which I should have.

"Why are you avoiding me?" someone asked.

"Who is this?"

"Nick."

"Leave me alone, Nick. Are you the one who's sending me letters and emailing me? How did you get those things?"

"I have my ways. Victor and I miss you."

"You and Victor both need to leave me alone."

I hung up and went to my father. I knocked on his door. "Daddy? Kristy?" I said, knocking softly.

"Come in," Kristy called.

"What's up?" my Dad said.

"I think I know who is stalking me."

"Who and why?"

"Nick Godejohn. He is my ex-boyfriend. I met him online and then in person. We had sex in the restroom of the movie theater, my idea not his, and before I left home, I broke up with him."

"I'll give his name to the police when I go tomorrow. From now on, just write down any time that an unknown number or email or message comes in. Just like you've been doing. The date and time. We'll get him."

"Thank you. Goodnight."

"Goodnight."

I said goodnight and went back to my room. I wouldn't put it past Nick to be outside my window, waiting for the lights to go out. So I made sure that my windows were locked and then I put a 2 by 4 in the window to make sure that he couldn't get in.

Chapter Twelve:

New Friends

After I had moved in with my father, making friends new friends had been very hard. I was really isolated when I was with my mother and she rarely let me out of the house or to talk to other people.

I was lucky enough to be able to speak with Laci. She was my neighbor had helped build the house that my mother and I had lived in.

"Hello," someone behind me said. "Are you new?"

My hair had grown in and I was so happy. Kristy had taken me shopping. I bought all kinds of headbands and hair ties and hair clips.

Hair brushes and combs. Some new clothes and things like that. The things that I liked.

It had been really fun. I think both Kristy and I had to take naps after we'd gotten back.

My hair was shoulder length, a chestnut brown and wavy. Not frizzy and curly like my mother's had been. I'd also had my feeding tube removed and was eating straight solid foods. I'd gained some weight. Nothing extreme.

"I started a couple of months ago," I said, easily. "I didn't have hair at the time."

"Oh, right," the boy said. "You look really pretty. I like dark hair."

"Thank you. I'm Gypsy Rose."

"Austin."

"Nice to meet you."

"You, too. Would you like to do something after school?"

"Sure."

I was going to the local community college. My stepmom would be picking me up.

"I just need to call my stepmom to let her know."

"Great. Meet me here after your last class."

"Okay."

"I'll get a small group together."

"Sounds fun."

I pulled out my cellphone on the way to my next class and called Kristy. "Hey, Kristy," I said, excitedly.

"Are you okay?" she asked.

"Yeah. I just met boy and he asked me to hang out after school I just wanted to let you know."

"How fun! Is it just the two of you?"

"No, he's going to get a small group of his friends together."

"Great. Have fun. Call if you need a ride home."

"I will. Thank you!"

"You're welcome."

I reached my class, turned off my cell, and took my seat. I was excited to see where the day led.

Chapter Thirteen:

After School

"You came," Austin said, walking up to me with about six other people.

"Sure," I said, nervous. "Why wouldn't I?"

"I don't know. Ready?"

"Yes."

]   "Great. You can sit up front with me. We'll have to take two cars."

"Sounds good."

I followed Austin to his car and he opened the door for me. Once he joined me and the others in the car, he started the car, and pulled out of the driveway.

"Where are we going?" I asked.

"Just to the mall. There's a nice food court there. Maybe the movies."

"I don't have any money."

"Don't worry about it. This time its on me. Next time, you can do it."

I nodded.

I didn't get those jobs either. I forgot to mention that, but they did recommend trying again. Told me that while they liked my personality and thought that I would do good, I just needed more experience. They suggested maybe getting a job at the school in the bookstore or office for experience.

I liked that and I work in the bookstore three days a week. I also work in the main office two days a week.

"Tell me about you," Austin said.

"I lived in Springfield until two months ago. I was in a wheelchair," I said.

"Wow."

"Yeah."

"What else?"

"I just started work in the office and in the bookstore. I'm working on getting my license and then a car."

"You don't drive?"

"No."

"How come?" one of Austin's friends asked. I think her name was Camille.

"My mother abused me my whole life. She beat me and mentally abused me. She kept me confined to a wheelchair and told me that I had several bad diseases. Ones that could kill me. She would shave my head every day and tell people that I was sixteen when I wasn't."

"Oh my," another friend of his said, Jamie, I think.

"Yep. When I finally got the courage to tell someone, I called my dad and then revealed the truth. It felt freeing. Satisfying. Then she killed herself."

"Jesus."

"Oh shit!"

"I miss her, and I felt really guilty. After talking to my Dad and stepmom, I know that it had nothing to do with me. I did what I had to do, to save myself."

"Right."

"Very brave of you."

"I don't think so, but my family and former friends do. I think it was selfish."

"Why?"

I shrugged. "I don't know. I know that I shouldn't feel that way. She abused me. My mother would chain me to the bed and leave me there for days on end. I endured so many unnecessary surgeries. I know that I'm better off."

"You miss her?"

"Yes."

"You're braver than I thought." Austin took my hand and looked at me. "It will be okay."

I looked at him and smiled.

Chapter Fourteen:

Austin

I have been hanging out with Austin and his friends nearly everyday after classes let out. The only times that I don't is when I work at the school's bookstore.

The office work is done during the school day. The bookstore is immediately after school and sometimes before school.

Tonight, was my first official date with him. It would be just Austin and myself. We were going to see a movie and then have dinner. Maybe dancing. Though, I told him that I might not be very good at it.

He chuckled and said he definitely wasn't any good at it, but it was still fun.

My dad and stepmom had met him a few times before. He would drop me off at home and walk me to the door. Dad would ask him to come in and he'd just hang out with us for dinner and a TV show or a game afterwards.

My parents and siblings really liked him and so did I.

The doorbell rang.

"He's here!" Mia called out. "I'll get the door!"

She ran down the hallway. "Hi, Austin!' she said. "She'll be right out."

I could hear him laugh and he said, "Thank you, Mia. How was your day?"

"Very long. I had a hard history test. I didn't like it, but I think I did okay."

"That's great. Maybe I could help you, if you need it."

"Really? Do you think Gypsy would help too?"

"Probably. Did you ask her?"

"No."

"Maybe you should."

"Sure!"

I heard her barrel down the hallway and fling open my door. "Will you help me study for history?" she asked. "Austin said he would help, too."

"Sure," I said, smiling. History hadn't been my best subject when I took my GED test, but I did pass. "I can do that."

"Yay!" She ran out of my room, leaving the door wide open, and yelling that I said I'd help her, too.

I was ready and left my room.

"Hey, Austin," I said.

"Hey," he said, smiling. "Ready?"

"Yes."

He told my Dad that he would have me home by ten and that if we were going to be late, he or I would call him.

"Thank you," my Dad said.

We left and headed off to see a movie. Not a Disney one either.

* * *

"Did you like the movie?" Austin asked.

We had gone to see *Furious 7*. "Yeah," I said. "I didn't realize that I liked action movies. Vin Diesel is hot."

He laughed. "A lot of females say that. I suppose he is."

"You're hot, too."

He smiled. "I think you're hot."

He leaned down and kissed me. I wasn't expecting that. I also wasn't expecting the reaction that I had either.

"Wow."

"Really hot. Did you want to go to dinner?"

"No."

"Did you want to park somewhere?"

"Yes."

"Nice."

We exited the movie theater and went to his car. Then he drove for about twenty minutes to a nice, secluded lake. "Very cool," I said. "It's nice and private."

"Want to make out?" Austin asked.

"Yes. Very much."

Austin went into the backseat and then helped me back there. He leaned over and began kissing me. I kissed him back.

His hands grabbed my breast and I moaned against his lips.

"Don't stop."

"What?"

"I don't want to stop. Go lower. Put your hands all over me."

"Sex?"

"Yes."

He kissed me again and then kept going like I asked.

Chapter Fifteen:

Nick Returns

When I arrived home, Austin walked me to the door and kissed me on the porch. Then he left, telling me he'd call when he got home.

I went into the house and my Dad was waiting up.

"Were you safe?" he asked.

"Daddy!" I exclaimed.

He looked at me. "Gypsy..."

"Yes, Daddy."

"Can we talk?"

"Of course."

I entered the living room and sat beside him. "What did you want to talk about?"

"I don't mind that you have sex, you're old enough. Just don't encourage Mia."

"Never. I don't talk to her about sex or boys. We talk about school and sister stuff like dolls and clothes. Hair things and make up."

"Okay, good. You were safe?"

"Yes, Daddy. He didn't pressure me or anything like that. I wanted to do it. I'm glad I did. I like him a lot. I see this going far."

"Good. Just be smart about. I know you are very smart."

My phone rang and it was Austin.

"One second, Daddy. It's Austin," I said. "He said that he would call when he got home."

My Dad smiled. "Go ahead," he said. "That's really nice of him."

"I know, I didn't think that he would. I know that guys will say they will call after you sleep together and they don't always do that."

"Very true."

I picked up the phone. "Austin?"

"Guess again," the male voice said. "It's Victor. You did a very bad thing."

"Nick?"

My Dad looked at me and grabbed his phone. I saw him dial 911 and begin talking quietly and urgently on the phone.

"Where is Austin, Nick?"

"I am not Nick. I am Victor."

"You are the same body, I know. I want to know what happened to Austin."

"He's dead."

I stared at my phone and felt it fall from my hands.

"What did he say?" my Dad asked.

I looked at my Dad, with haunted eyes, I'm sure. "He said Austin is dead."

Chapter Sixteen:

Austin is Gone

It has been months since Austin was murdered by my ex-boyfriend. I testified against Nick. His attorney said that he wasn't mentally competent enough to go to trial, the judge and state mental health officials thought differently.

I told the court what I knew, which wasn't much. I told them that I had dated Nick in Springfield. That we had met online and talked for a couple of years before meeting up at the movie theater. I told them that we had sex in the restroom.

Then I told them that after my mother had died, I broke up with him. I also told them that when I had broken up with him, he had begun stalking me.

When that was done, I told them that he had called me from my boyfriend's phone, I had asked him where Austin was and he had said he was dead.

The officers had arrived and found him on the phone with me, standing over Austin's body. There wasn't anything that could have been done.

I am pregnant by Austin.

My Dad asked me, when I told him, about being safe. I told him that Austin had put on a condom and it must have had a hole in it.

His parents, Austin's wanted a DNA test, which I readily agreed to. I knew it was Austin's baby. They did an amniocentesis to prove it. It is Austin's baby.

I told his parents that I loved Austin and that if I had known that Nick was lurking around that I never would have put him any danger.

They believed me.

I will give birth to his son. I am doing to name him after his father.

Afterword

My little boy, Austin Ever Gaines Blanchard, was born three weeks early. He is a little fighter and I know that Austin is looking down on us.

In a surprise twist, Austin's cousin came up for his service and we are now dating. It was a little weird at first. I know that we all thought so, but it felt right.

Austin's parents are supportive of the relationship and so are my parents. They think it will be good to have someone around for the baby.

I moved out of my Dad's house and into a small, but nice apartment nearby. Halfway between his house and Austin's parents' house.

I want them all to be involved. I don't want to be like my mother. Austin's cousin lives with me.

Little Austin will be home in a few weeks, he's making great strides and I couldn't be happier.

I did have my name legally changed. I was born Gypsy Rose Blanchard and I will now live my life as Emma Rose Blanchard. At least, until I get married.

Update

As of this writing, the actual Gypsy Rose Blanchard is serving a ten-year sentence for second degree murder at Missouri's Chillicothe Correctional Center.

Recent reports also say that she is engaged to a man that she met through a prison pen pal program and are waiting to be married until after she is released from prison. The earliest possible release date is in 2023. Though family and others are trying to get her released earlier.

Her ex-boyfriend, Nick Godejohn, is serving a life sentence. He was convicted of first-degree murder and will never see the outside of prison.

About the Author

Marie was born in Modesto, California in September of 1981 and raised in Vancouver, Washington. She graduated high school from Prairie High School in Brush Prairie, Washington in June of 2000. In January of 2006 she graduated college from Everest College (formerly Western Business College) in Vancouver, Washington.

She was raised by her maternal grandparents and has four half-sisters and three half-brothers.

Marie married in the fall of 2010 and they reside in Washougal, Washington.

Delta Files

The Hotel Slayings

The Masked Killer

Ballerina

Recreational Murder

Fake

Trea-Bella Donna

Vacay

Trea-Bella Donna: Prison Queen

Suicide Killer

State Route

Coroner

Addyson

Broken

Redemption

Addyson Private Investigations

Kaula Dawkins

Adam Corning

Pami Simpson

Untold Stories

Haden Delta, Volume 1

Tessa Kellogg

Poetry Collections

Bored and Bleeding

Egotistical Mama

Powerful Desire

From Me to You

Blood Speaks

Remembrance

Sinking Freely

Weeping Summer

Coast to Coast

Short Story Collections

The Scorned American

A Perfectly Secret Affair

The Haunted Third Shift

Lonely Nights and Crimson Lips

Worlds Apart and Then Some

Second Sapphire

Deadly

Key Moments

2 in 1 Novels

Espionage Garden

Hotels Unmasked

Recreational Ballet

A Marvelous Black Death

Vacant Queen

Killer State

The Duo

The Ending

For Better or Worse

Other Novels

Dew

Weird

Twelve Months

Better Days

Espionage: An American Tale

The Garden

Dreamland Theater

Almost Amish

Come Travel with Me

Black Widow

A Far Worse Place (Vol. 1)

Wastelands

A Better Worse Place (Vol. 2)

The Expectant Mother

The Photography Sessions

The Evil Ones